W9-AGF-288

WATERS

Edith Newlin Chase

Ron Broda

FIREFLY BOOKS

Sprinkling, wrinkling,
softly tinkling,

twinkling tiny brook,

running, funning,
hiding, sunning,

cunning baby brook,

joins a grown-up brook.

Dashing, splashing,
sunlight flashing,
stony grown-up brook,

13

joins the river,
broad smooth river,

deep as deep can be.

Slower, slower, slower flowing,

wider, wider, wider growing,

till it empties all its waters out
into the great huge sea.

Rolling, rolling,
tossing, rolling,

22

splashing waves forever rolling
in the great wide sea.

23

To Lyra and Larsson,
Michael and Isobel,
and other children who love
streams and the sea.
E.N.C.

For my brothers and sisters:
Bob, Tom, Terry, Connie, Crystal,
Fred, Kevin, Kim, Todd and Brigit.
Also in loving memory of our father,
Fred Broda.
R.B.

Photography by William Kuryluk.
The illustrations for this book were done with paper
sculpture and watercolour. Each layer was cut, formed
and painted before being glued into place.

A FIREFLY BOOK

Published 1995 in the United States by:
Firefly Books (U.S.) Inc.
P.O. Box 1338
Ellicott Station
Buffalo, New York
14207

Text copyright © 1993 by Edith Newlin Chase
Illustrations copyright © 1993 by Ron Broda
Published by arrangement with North Winds Press.

Cataloguing in Publication Data

Chase, Edith Newlin
Waters

A poem.
ISBN 1-895565-77-4

1. Water — Juvenile poetry. 2. Children's poetry,
American. I. Broda, Ron. II. Title.

PZ8.3.358.Wa 1996   j811'.54   C95-931354-0

No part of this publication may be reproduced or stored in a retrieval system, or
transmitted any form or by any means, electronic, mechanical, photocopying, recording or
otherwise, without the written permission of the publisher, Firefly Books.

Printed and bound in Canada

About this book

All creatures need water, but they use it in different ways. Some merely sip from a tiny drop of melted snow. Others need the space of huge oceans in which to roam. In this book, you can find creatures that make their homes in the water, on the water or by the water. There are creatures that live in the water but breathe air. There are creatures that live and breathe water, all their lives. And there are those that spend some of their time in water and some on land, needing both to survive.

Many of the creatures pictured in this book depend on water for their food. They might hunt over the water, in the water, on the water's surface or beside the water. Even grazing creatures need water, for it nourishes the plants they eat.

The creatures in the book are:

• (endpapers) belugas • (title page) dragonfly • (2-3) snowshoe hare, chickadees, bald eagle, cedar waxwing • (4-5) feild mouse, northern leopard bullfrog, snail, red-spotted purple moth, common garden spider, ladybugs • (6-7) tree squirrel, bison, raccoon, pronghorns, ruby-throated hummingbird, kingbird, green snake, bumblebee • (8-9) horses, prairie dog, meadowlark, grasshopper • (10-11) caribou, lemming, goldeneyes, red-wing blackbird, brooktrout, water striders, mosquito • (12-13) chipmunk, black bear, belted kingfisher, brook trout, dragonfly • (14-15) white-tailed deer, great blue heron, Canada geese, green frog, viceroy butterfly, nuthatches • (16-17) moose, yellow warbler, loons, ladybug, praying mantis, black-fly, caterpillar • (18-19) blue jay • (20-21) harbour seals, herring gulls, puffins • (22-23) bottlenose dolphins, humpback whale • (copyright page) Canada geese.